Oscar
needs a
Friend

Scholastic Children's Books,
Commonwealth House, 1-19 New Oxford Street,
London WC1A 1NU, UK
a division of Scholastic Ltd
London ~ New York ~ Toronto ~ Sydney ~ Auckland

Published by Scholastic Ltd, 1998

Text copyright © Joan Stimson, 1998
Illustrations copyright © Meg Rutherford, 1998

ISBN: 0 590 54331 8

Printed in Hong Kong

Oscar
needs a
Friend

by Joan Stimson

Illustrated by Meg Rutherford

SCHOLASTIC
PRESS

Oscar was a bear who couldn't keep still.
All day long he raced round the mountainside.

At bedtime he raced round Mum.

And when at last he snuggled down, Oscar
always said the same thing.
"I wish there were more bears on our side of
the mountain. And I wish there was another
bear who liked the same sort of games as me!"

Weeks passed and Oscar wondered if he
would ever find a friend.

Then one day he bounded home, bursting with excitement.

"Mum, Mum," cried Oscar. "Some new bears have moved in . . . just up the track. And the little one looks as if he needs a friend too."

The new little bear was called Ollie. And
straight after lunch Oscar set off to meet him.

"Let's play on my slide," said Oscar. And, without waiting for a reply, he pulled Ollie to the top of his favourite bank.

"Isn't this great!" cried Oscar, as the two bears tumbled down the bank together.

But Ollie wasn't so sure. And before long
he scuttled back to his mum.

That evening at supper Oscar was sulky. But next day he went to see Ollie again.

"Let's play on my bouncy branch," said Oscar. And, without waiting for a reply, he pushed Ollie up into his favourite tree.

"Isn't this great!" cried Oscar, as the
two bears tried to balance in the breeze.

But Ollie wasn't so sure. And before long he
scuttled back to his mum.

That night at story time Oscar stomped about.

But next day he went to see Ollie again.
"Let's play hide-and-seek," said Oscar.

And, without waiting for a reply,
he ran off and left Ollie in the
dark and gloomy wood.

"Isn't this great!" hollered Oscar from
a distance. But Ollie was already wailing.
"I want to go home . . . *now*!"

That night at bedtime Oscar had a tantrum.

"Ollie says my slide's too steep, my branch
is too bouncy and my wood's too scary,"
he yelled. "And he keeps running home to
his mum."

When at last she could make herself heard,
Oscar's mum made a suggestion.

Oscar pretended not to listen. But before
he went to sleep, he thought about what
Mum had said.

And next morning he raced round to Ollie's home.

"What would *you* like to do today?" asked Oscar. Then he waited patiently for a reply.

At first there was a stunned silence. But next there was a *whooooosh!* And Ollie bounced out from behind his mum.

"Swimming!" he announced. And the two bears
ran eagerly towards the water.
Oscar watched in amazement as Ollie
scrambled up to the highest rock.
And leapt straight in.

"We had a huge lake at my old home," explained Ollie.

All morning the two bears splashed and whooped in the water.

That afternoon Ollie asked if he could try
Oscar's slide again. And then his branch.
"It's easier than I thought," beamed Ollie.

"I do hope he'll want to play hide-and-seek soon," thought Oscar to himself. But he knew now that he must wait until Ollie was ready.

"And what do you think of your new friend today?" asked Mum, when it was time to take Ollie home.

"I think that Ollie is *brilliant*!" cried Oscar.
"And that I am the luckiest bear on the
mountain."